This book belongs to

_____

This educational book was created in cooperation with Children's Television Workshop, producers of SESAME STREET. Children do not have to watch the television show to benefit from this book. Workshop revenues from this book will be used to help support CTW educational projects.

ON MY WAY WITH SESAME STREET

Volume 5

All About Me

Featuring the Sesame Street Characters
Children's Television Workshop / Funk & Wagnalls

Authors

Stephanie Calmenson
Linda Hayward
Emily Perl Kingsley
David Korr
Michaela Muntean

Illustrators

Richard Brown
Tom Cooke
A. Delaney
Tom Leigh
Maggie Swanson
Richard Walz
Marsha Winborn

0-8343-0079-6

1 2 3 4 5 6 7 8 9 0

A Parents' Guide to ALL ABOUT ME

One of the most important things a child can learn is self-esteem. Pride in oneself and a sense of accomplishment make a preschooler feel confident as he or she faces the challenges of growing up.

Sometimes, a new experience can seem threatening. This book introduces your children to social and emotional milestones most children encounter. After hearing about Bert going to the doctor or Betty Lou staying with a baby-sitter for the first time, your children will feel more comfortable when they find themselves in the same predicament. They'll know what to expect. Talking about the new experience helps, too.

''I Can Do It Myself'' shows Sesame Street friends performing such preschool tasks as pouring juice, pulling on boots, climbing to the top of the jungle gym, setting the table, and more.

''The Truth About Monsters'' uses reassurance and humor to help children deal with common childhood fears. When Grover thinks there's a monster under the bed, all he finds is dust!

In ''First Times,'' your children will see Baby Monster taking her first step, Malcolm Monster getting his first fur-cut, and Ernie and Bert taking care of their first pet.

''Words About Feelings'' is just one activity that will encourage your children to express their own feelings.

ALL ABOUT ME will help your children on the road to learning all about themselves.

The Editors
SESAME STREET BOOKS

I Think
That It Is
Wonderful

I think that it is wonderful
to wake up with the sun
when it has just begun
to shine.
Hello, bright morning sun.

I think that it is wonderful
to hear the waking street
as all those busy feet
go by.
Hello, Sesame Street.

Me think that it is wonderful
to wake up wanting food.
To be in hungry mood
is swell.
(Don't worry, my tummy stop growling
after me have breakfast.)
Hello, food food food food!

I think that it is wonderful
to stretch from head to heels.
When I get up it feels
just right.
Hello, knees, toes, and heels.

I think that it is wonderful
to scrub each part of me
to make sure I will be
all clean.
Hello, clean, spiffy me.

I Can Do It Myself

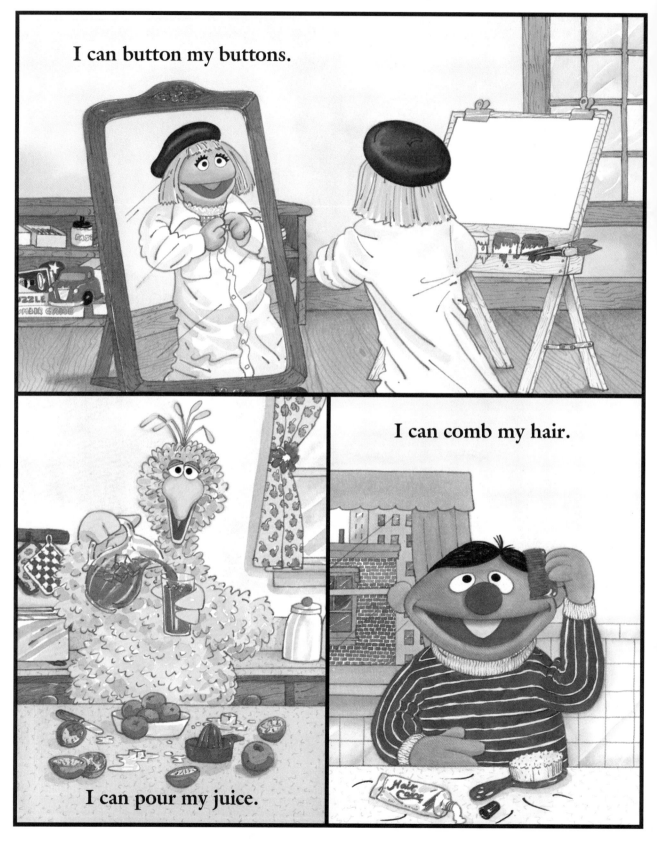

I can button my buttons.

I can comb my hair.

I can pour my juice.

I can set the table.

I can carry my plate to
the kitchen sink.

Bert Goes to the Doctor

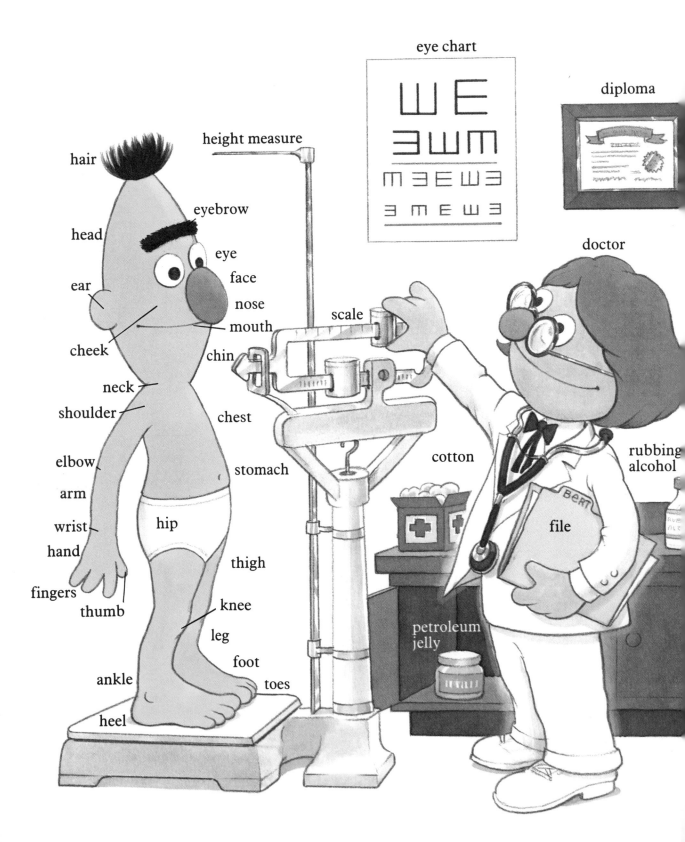

eye chart

diploma

hair

height measure

eyebrow

head

eye

face

ear

nose

scale

doctor

mouth

cheek

chin

neck

shoulder

chest

cotton

rubbing
alcohol

elbow

stomach

arm

file

wrist

hip

hand

thigh

fingers

knee

thumb

leg

foot

petroleum
jelly

ankle

toes

heel

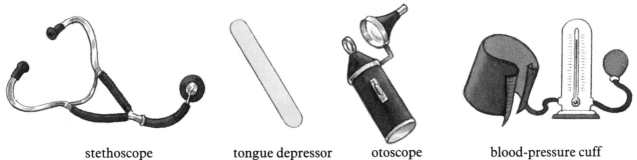

stethoscope   tongue depressor   otoscope   blood-pressure cuff

During Bert's checkup, the doctor . . .

listens to Bert's heart,

looks in Bert's ears

and down his throat,

tests Bert's eyesight,

tests Bert's reflexes,

takes Bert's blood pressure

and temperature,

and gives Bert a shot to help keep him well.

      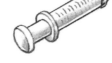   

flashlight   reflex hammer   hypodermic needle   thermometer

The Truth About Monsters

Hello, everybodee! It is I, lovable, furry old Grover
Monster. Did you know that some people have very silly
ideas about monsters? Oh, it is true—and it is terrible!
That is why I am here to tell you the *truth* about monsters.

First of all, many people think that monsters are big
and ugly and scary.

Now look at my friend Herry. It is true that he is big. It
is true that he is not as cute and adorable as I am. But he
is not scary. Are you, Herry?

Herry may not be a scary monster, but he is a scary
ghost!

Many people think that monsters like to hide in closets and under beds at night. This is ridiculous.

Look at this closet. It is a mess. Would you like to stand in there with all that junk? I will show you how silly that would be.

I was right. That was silly.

Now look under this bed. No monster with any sense
would hide under there, because he would get dustballs in
his fur. Here, I will show you!

I, Grover Monster, was right again. Excuse me while I go
take a bath.

Hello again. It is I, lovable, furry old *clean* Grover. I am back to tell you more truths about monsters.

Some people think that monsters like to hide behind bushes and then jump out and scare you. This is another silly idea. Look at this bush. Do you think there is a monster behind it?

Uh-oh. That big green bush said something. Oh, my goodness! It is not a bush. It is a big furry green monster! Please forgive my monstrous mistake.

The green bush, er…monster has asked me to stay and play with him. He is waiting for his mommy because he is not old enough to walk home alone.

So the next time someone tells you about monsters, you can say that you already know the *truth* about monsters!

So Many Things

So many things,
So many, many things to do,
Too many for one day,
Too many for my little feet
To take me all that way;
Too many for my little hands,
My little eyes and ears;
But tomorrow I will start again.
I'm afraid this may take years.

Frazzle Goes to the Dentist

During Frazzle's checkup the dentist looks
for cavities, cleans and counts Frazzle's teeth,
and shows him the right way to brush them.

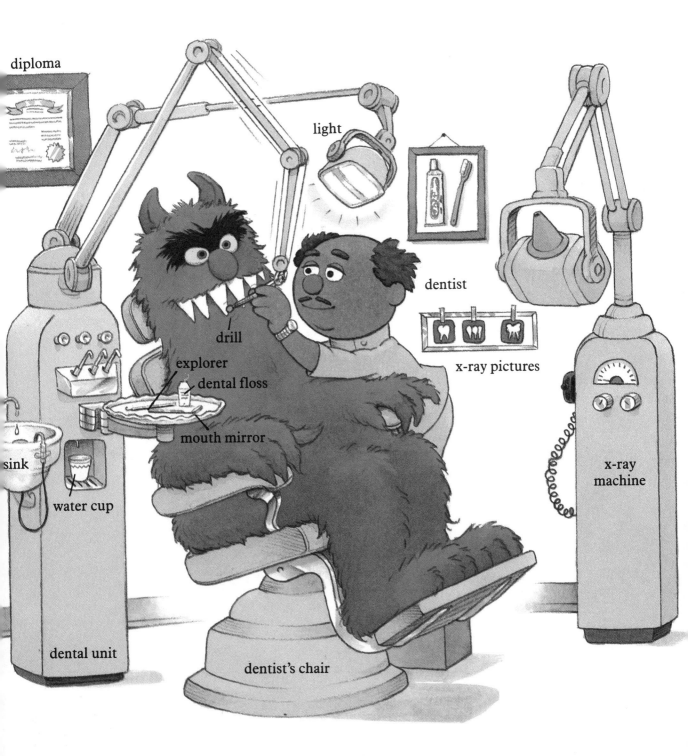

diploma

light

dentist

x-ray pictures

drill

explorer

dental floss

mouth mirror

sink

x-ray machine

water cup

dental unit

dentist's chair

Bert has found a rock.
He is **excited**.
Ernie is **bored**.

Big Bird has stepped
on Herry's toe.
Big Bird is **sorry**.
Herry is **angry**.

Telly has dropped his
backpack into the stream.
He is **sad**.

Words About Feelings

Scout Leader Grover and his friends are taking a hike in the woods. How would you feel if Big Bird stepped on your toe?

Betty Lou has climbed a hill. She is **proud**.

Barkley has bumped into a beehive. He is **worried**.

Grover has found some wildflowers. He is **happy**.

Farley wants to cross the stream. He is **afraid**.

Prairie Dawn has discovered a rabbit family. She is **surprised**.

Little by Little

Little by little,
I'm getting bigger.
I grow every day.
I can reach the
kitchen counter.

I can sit at the table
without a telephone book
to make me taller.

I can swing
without getting
a push.

I can get my own
cup of water when
I wake up.

Little by little, I'm getting bigger!

The Mirror Poem

No mirror's big enough for Snuff
   to see all Snuff at once.
He could try doing it in bits,
   but that would take him months.
So I walk all around him
   and tell him what I see.
And then, because he is my friend,
   he does the same for me.

I HAVE A FRIEND

I have lots of friends. When we play hide-and-seek, I cover my eyes and all my friends hide.

My friend Bird comes to visit me when have a cold. He makes me feel better.

My friend Grover does funny things. He cheers me up when I feel sad. Yuh.

I have a friend who likes to count
almost as much as I do.
One friend and one friend
make two. Ha! Ha! Ha!

My old buddy Bert
likes me even when
I make him
look silly.

I have a friend who will lend me
whatever I need, even if
it's brand-new.

I have a friend who pops up
whenever I need him.

I, Grover, have a friend who helps me try new things. Oh, my goodness! It is not easy to be a skating star!

My friend Ernie makes me feel brave even when he's scared, too.

I have two friends who invite me to stay for supper. I wish they didn't always serve birdseed stew.

Friends are yucchy. I tell them
to go away and leave me alone.

But I don't mind when they bring me
a cake and wish me a rotten birthday.

My friend and I like to share sodas at Mr. Hooper's store.

My friend Barkley always meets me after school. He's very happy to see me.

My friend Ernie is a good sport. And he doesn't even mind when I win.

My friend Herry calls me every day.
We have a lot to talk about.

My friend Sully and I eat lunch
together every day. I'm glad
we're pals.

My friends and I have lots of fun whenever we're together.
Do you have good friends, too?

Oh, I Was So Embarrassed!

Have you ever been embarrassed?

Have you ever felt so foolish
You just wished to run away?
"Why, yes!" you cry? Then hear how I
Embarrassed ME today.

I took the bus all by myself,
In my little coat and cap.
I felt so proud, until I sat
On someone else's lap!

"Oh, no!" I said. "What have I done?
Would you excuse me, please?
I should have looked before I sat
And landed on your knees!"

The woman on whose lap I perched
Was, oh, so very kind.
She told me that she understood,
She really did not mind.

I said, "Oh, thank you very much.
You have not frowned a bit.
You under*stand* I did not mean
To make you under*sit!*"

With that I stood up hurriedly
And found another place.
Embarrassment most certainly
Was painted on my face.

Since you have felt embarrassed, too,
I do not have to say
How glad I am that I found out
The feeling goes away!

When I Grow Up

One day all the kids in the class dressed up like people
in the neighborhood.

What would Bert like to be when he grows up?
What does everybody else want to be?

First Times

The first time Herry Monster rode the school bus, he sat by a window so he could wave to his mommy.

When Malcolm Monster went to get his first fur-cut, he didn't know what to expect.

Afterward, Malcolm looked very handsome.

The first time that the Amazing Mumford tried to do a magic trick . . .

it was truly amazing!

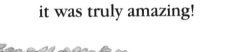

The first time Grover wrote his name all by himself, he wanted everyone to see it.

The first time Prairie Dawn wore party shoes, she didn't want to take them off.

The first time Ernie spent a whole dollar by himself, he bought a notebook, a giant pencil, and a present for Bert.

The first time Bert went to the library, he couldn't decide which book to borrow.

When Baby Monster took her first step, her big brother, Herry, was there to help.

The first mystery Sherlock Hemlock ever solved was The Case of the Missing Kite.

The first night Barkley spent on Sesame Street was the night Ernie and Bert learned how to take care of a puppy.

The first time the Honkers went to a concert, the conductor asked them to please be quiet!

When Betty Lou stayed with a baby-sitter for the first time, she listened to her favorite story three times in a row.

There are always new things to try for the very first time. Oops! Try again, Big Bird.

Hurray!
Now, what would you like to try for the very first time?

I Think That It Is Wonderful

I think that it is wonderful
that I can see a star,
when it's so very far
away.
Good night, faraway star.

I think that it is wonderful
that I can hear birds sing,
when outside everything
is still.
Good night, bird on the wing.

Me think that it is wonderful
to eat my food all up,
especially at sup-
per time.
(Or lunch time or breakfast time.
It not matter.)
Night, night, delicious food.

I think that it is wonderful
that I can smell a rose.
I'm so glad that my nose
knows how.
Good night, sweet-smelling rose.

I think that it is wonderful
to hug my Teddy bear.
It doesn't matter where
we are.
Sleep tight, Teddy, my bear.

Good night, faraway star.
Good night, bird on the wing.
Good night, delicious food.
Good night, sweet-smelling rose.
Good night, Teddy, my bear.

Good night, good night, good night.